Colours

Written by
Alice Hemming

Look at this picture.

This picture has many colours in it.

You can make all the colours in this picture from just three colours: red, yellow and blue.

Primary colours

We call red, yellow and blue **primary colours.**

Red

Yellow

Blue

We can mix these three colours to make new colours.

Red and yellow make orange.

Yellow and blue make green.

Blue and red make purple.

Secondary colours

We call orange, green and purple **secondary colours**. They are made from other colours.

Orange
Green
Purple

We can mix orange, green and purple to make more colours.

Red mixed with orange makes red-orange.

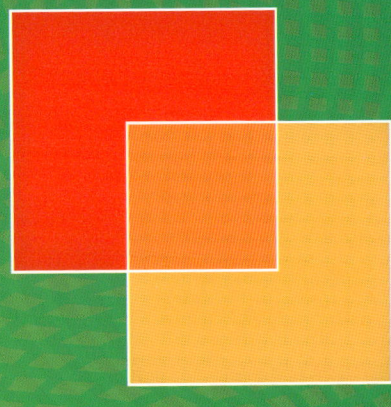

Yellow mixed with green makes yellow-green.

Blue mixed with purple makes blue-purple.

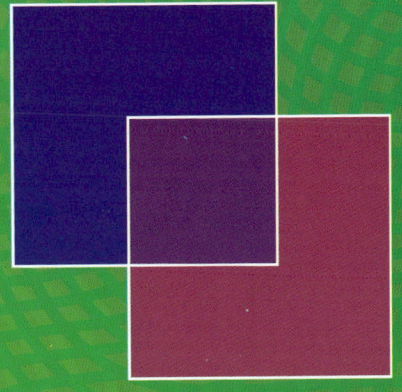

Warm colours

We call red, orange and yellow warm colours.

These are the colours of fire and the Sun. These colours make you feel warm.

This picture has lots of warm colours.

Cool colours

We call blue, purple and green cool colours.

They are the colours of water and the night. These colours can make you feel cool, or even cold.

This picture has lots of cool colours.

The colour wheel

This is a colour wheel. It shows what happens when we mix different colours.

On this colour wheel, the colours are lighter nearer the middle of the wheel and darker nearer the outside.

Opposite colours

The colours that are facing each other on the colour wheel work well together.

These opposite colours work well together:

- ✓ blue and orange
- ✓ red and green
- ✓ purple and yellow.

Colours on the opposite sides of the colour wheel can help each other.

We like to look at these colours next to each other.

This picture uses the opposite colours of red and green.

There are many thousands of different colours. They are all made from red, yellow and blue.